HAVE A LITTLE FAITH

K.O. NEWMAN

 Created with Vellum

For my found family, who make every holiday a little extra special.

1

Faith

I watched the clouds float by my window as I fingered the smooth skin at the bottom of my left ring finger, a nervous habit that I picked up when I had still worn my rings and I could spin my wedding band around my finger. There was something almost satisfying about not having that weight on my hand. It was freeing. At least that's what I was telling myself. And what Birdie had been trying to drill into my head ever since my mild breakdown at Thanksgiving. I was only a little drunk. Promise.

I tipped back the last of the whiskey in my little plastic cup that held the most watered down Jameson and ginger ale I ever had. The ice clicked against my teeth as the airplane dipped, along with my stomach.

If you had asked me about this all-inclusive surprise Christmas getaway when I booked it for my husband and I six months ago, I would have told you all about the little island in the Caribbean we were going to. The cute little cabana on the beach I had booked. The couples massage, the parties on the beach, and how much I couldn't wait to try out the hot tub that our adorable cabin had.

Now?

I'm divorced.

I didn't see it coming either. Gavin and I were happy. At Least I thought we were. But then I got home from work, and he's on the couch, hands folded in his lap, and the tickets for the trip were sitting on the table next to him along with the ripped envelope. And then he said those dreaded four words.

"Faith." He sighed and looked just over my left shoulder, like he couldn't even stand to look me in the eye. "We have to talk."

By Halloween we were living separately. He *generously* let me have the house, like it hadn't been my inheritance that had bought it in the first place. By Thanksgiving, I was signing the divorce papers. The entire time my surprise Christmas vacation tickets and itinerary sat on the side table in my living room, mocking me.

I could still feel the thousand dollar Mont Blanc pen my lawyer handed me, while Gavin and his lawyer sat on the other side of the palatial ebony conference table. It felt like it weighed a hundred pounds as I signed my name on the line under Respondent. Crossing the T in my name and then dotting the I, I felt like my insides had turned to stone. Gavin's signature looked so satisfied, and mine looked like it was bleeding from the wounds that my husband - the man I vowed to love honor and cherish - had left on my heart.

I spent Black Friday returning gifts. Ironic, I know. The only one I couldn't take back? The trip. The one where I was going to tell Gavin that I was finally ready to start trying to have a family. The reason he had asked for the divorce in the first place. Because he didn't want to have a family with me. Not after I had put it off for so long - three years, give me a fucking break - he had found someone else who wanted a family right away.

Everything changed so fast. I felt like I had whiplash. But my best friend Birdie told me to embrace it. Take the trip I had planned so carefully, and say fuck you to Gavin and his slutty secretary - I'm sorry, administrative assistant - who were expecting their first child together.

I embraced Birdie's suggestion and took the vacation. I pulled my phone out from my bag and sent her a quick text, just saying good morning. Her immediate response of good followed by about a million hearts made my aching heart ease a little. She always had my back.

Then I looked up to see the young couple in front of me sharing a sweet kiss. I was gonna need another drink before we landed.

Dash

I kicked my feet up and surveyed the beach from the cabin my buddies and I rented. Just one week. We had one week of leave until our next big op, and I planned on enjoying every minute.

I laced my hands behind my head and scanned the beach for some chick to relieve the deep down tension that coursed through me. We had one major operation a year, and while physically I was at the top of my game, that assignment required nothing less than absolute concentration and commitment. And my head just wouldn't focus on the girls on the beach. It was somewhere else entirely.

There had been this little niggling in the back of my mind all day that I couldn't get rid of. Something was riling my animal up, and the beach was not the place to Change. Especially into my beast.

So, I scanned the beach looking for someone to take the edge off with.

There were plenty of single women who I could lose myself in for a night or two. Once the week was over, we wouldn't be back for an entire year, and most of these babes wouldn't be coming back, anyway.

"What do you think? Blonde or brunette?" Cupid handed me an ice-cold bottle of beer before dropping down next to me and twisting the top off his own . "I'm in the mood for a redhead, I think."

"Am I that predictable?" I tapped the neck of my beer against his and took a long pull from the bottle.

"It's what we're here for, right? Gotta knock off all this dust and bust a nut or six before we head out." Cupid pushed his aviators up the bridge of his nose and slunk down in his seat. "That's what the General told us to do."

"He did not tell us to, and I quote, 'Bust a nut or six.'" Vix growled from behind his tablet. Probably going over mission briefs again. If I didn't love the guy so much, I would hate the fucking brown noser. "I don't know about you boys, but when I decide to 'bust a nut,' as you so eloquently put it, it's going to be with a woman who is worth my time and effort to do it right."

"Ugh! Come on, man." Cupid threw his head back and moaned. "Christ Vix. Not this waiting for your perfect mate crap again. With our schedule, we're gonna be good for a quickie . We aren't gonna be no good to some chicks - who will be stuck with us, by the way. With missions and training, we are *rarely* at home."

"The right one will be perfect for our lives." Vix insisted, finally putting down his fucking tablet. "She will be exactly what I need. That is how the mating bond works."

"Come on." I rolled my eyes, knowing he couldn't see them behind my shades. "The three of us would have to find the same mate, just to keep her happy year round. And what's some poor girl going to tell her family when we're never home for Christmas? Cause you know, we never will be. Like ever."

"Have a little faith, Dash." Vix rolled his shoulders and picked his tablet back up, slouching down low in his beach chair and crossing his legs before burying his nose back in the tablet.

"I wouldn't mind sharing with you two." Was all Cupid said before jumping to his feet. "I need another beer. You guys good?"

I tipped my beer back, letting the alcohol flow down my throat as I continued to scan the beach. I had no problem sharing with my brothers at arms. It's not like we hadn't done it before. It was fun for a night. What woman wouldn't want three strapping special ops boys taking care of her every need for a little while? Would it work long term? No idea. But I felt that little nagging bit of longing grow in my chest. Fucking Vix.

2

Faith

My little cabin looked directly out onto the beach. Not a single tree obscured the breathtaking view of the ocean, and what I was told to be Angel Cay, which was owned by some rock star, apparently. Must be nice.

The breeze that swept off the water smelled like paradise. The tantalizing scent of salty sea, coconut oil, and something else that tickled my senses. Something warm and spicy that I couldn't identify.

I settled down in a beach chair and kicked my feet up on the little table that sat out on my porch. I already felt better. Much better than I expected. Maybe, for once, Birdie was right. I took a sip of my morning coffee and picked up my Kindle.

Just a little shifter romance before I started my day. Being divorced and on my romantic getaway alone would not interrupt my morning ritual.

As I drank my coffee, I felt the rest of the cay wake up. The sounds of people moving about filtered across the island and brought back the anxiety of being alone. I'd never been anywhere alone. I had gone from my parents' house to college, then I got married. I had never lived by myself, let alone gone on vacation solo.

Birdie said it would be a wonderful change, I reminded myself. And I was already enjoying the tranquility with my morning coffee on the beach. It was so different from the quiet of the house first thing in the morning; that kind of quiet felt empty. On the beach, it was full of life. I shook out my shoulders and picked my Kindle back up. It was going to be fine.

I finished my coffee to the rhythm of lumberjack bear shifters finding their perfect mates. And a bit of watching the early beach-goers settling in. I even took a break to watch as three extremely well-proportioned men ran down the beach together.

Just appreciating the view.

There was an odd pull below my belly as I watched their tight backsides disappear from view. A warmth in places that had seen no action from anyone but me in months.

And it had been months. Longer than just the separation and the divorce proceedings. There were so many red flags that I had ignored. I shook my head and gathered up my Kindle and empty coffee cup. I was heading back inside when out of nowhere, I hit a brick wall.

Cupid

She was perfect.

That was the only thought I had in my head as I steadied the little minx that had collided with me.

She was adorable.

A pert little nose nestled just over lush, warm lips. Lips that I wanted to bite. I wanted to sink my teeth into the pillowy softness of that pouty bottom lip and never let go.

"Oh, gosh." Her hands came up to push at my chest. I hadn't even realized that I was still holding her. "I'm so sorry. Good thing I finished my coffee already."

I slowly let her out of my embrace. Just making sure she was steady on her feet, I told myself. But then the breeze kicked up and brought with it the most beautiful scent as it ruffled her long brown locks. My animal sat up and kicked at my insides.

Mate.

No, man. I pushed him back down and shook my head. We're not made for a mate.

Mate.

I huffed and fought down the urge to pull her back into my arms. I watched as she bent and started picking up the broken pieces of her mug. "Shit." I dropped to my knees and took the sharp ceramic shards from her. "I didn't even see you."

"No, it's completely my fault." The scent of cinnamon and vanilla teased at my senses as she let me take the shattered shards from her hands. Her skin was like silk beneath my rough fingertips. "I didn't look where I was going."

"Well, my dear, I believe we are at an impasse." I gathered the last of the pieces into my hand and stood. "Let me take you to lunch, just to apologize."

"Oh." Shock colored her porcelain skin, with just a hint of a blush creeping up her neck to her cheeks. God, she was beautiful. "That's unnecessary." She reached back for the ceramic fragments in my hand, but I pulled it back from her reach.

"I insist."

"Will you give me the mug back if I agree?" She folded her arms across her chest and raised a brow. Danger Will Robinson. I robotically handed her the jagged pieces.

"Nope, just want lunch with a fetchingly beautiful woman." I dusted off my hands and shoved one in my pocket. "If it makes you feel better, my buddies can join us."

"I can't have lunch with you." She stooped and grabbed her tablet. "We don't know each other."

"And what better way to make new friends than to share a meal?" What the fuck? I sounded like Vix. I shook my head, and I held out a hand. "My friends call me Cupid."

She looked at my hand for a moment, hesitating, and then burst out laughing. "That's the worst pickup line ever."

"Not a pickup line." I winked at her as she abruptly stopped laughing. She eyed me suspiciously. I shrugged and kept my hand out for her to take. "It's my name. Well, my call sign."

"Military?" she asked, finally putting her hand in mine. I curled my fingers around her small hand and didn't want to let go.

"Something like that." I grinned when she didn't pull her fingers from mine. "And you are?"

She stared down at our joined hands, swallowing hard. That pretty blush coming back up and dusting her cheeks. "Faith." Her ocean blue eyes finally met mine, and my animal rolled over to show her his belly. He wanted her. Wanted her touch, her scent, all over our skin. "I'm Faith. It's nice to meet you Cupid." Faith took her hand out of mine, and I instantly felt the loss. "Now, if you'll excuse me, I need to get rid of this." She held up the broken mug and went to leave.

I caught her elbow and spun her back to me. "Please come have lunch with me and my friends." The scent of cinnamon was addling my brain. My animal was all but pawing at my chest, making my heart slam hard as I looked down at her. "Just lunch."

"Okay." Faith said a little breathlessly. "Just lunch."

"Good." I squeezed her arm where I still held it and grinned. My animal settled inside of me.

We had secured a date with our mate.

Not our mate, I insisted, but he just ignored me.

"I'll pick you up at noon." Fuck, I was a goner.

3

Faith

What the hell was I thinking? I couldn't go to lunch with a stranger. I threw the tenth tank top down on the bed and huffed, fisting my hands into my hips. Not only did I not know him, but I had nothing to wear.

Okay, that was a lie. I had plenty to wear. But what did a slightly too curvy woman wear to lunch with a built, crazy attractive man I didn't know, and his friends? I eyed the colorful array of clothing that adorned my king sized bed. There were tank tops and t-shirts, bikinis and coverups, jeans, cutoffs, and two cute flippy skirts that I was sure Birdie packed. Actually, I'm sure she packed the bikinis too, because they were all too skimpy for me. Conspicuously absent? My sensible one piece suit.

I picked up a cute, hot pink tank top and held it in front of my naked body, trying to ignore the fact that my hips are too wide, and my belly is more than a little soft. I sighed and threw it back on the bed.

Fuck.

Cupid had lured me into this impossible trap by being sexy and cute, and smoldering at me. My ovaries just couldn't take it. Not with such a recent dismissal from the man that was supposed to love me unconditionally. The heat in Cupid's eyes had done wonders to boost my confidence, though. And now I was second - and third and fourth - guessing everything.

I star-fished my body on the bed, disturbing mounds of clothing. I lay naked, staring up at the ceiling fan, which looked like it had palm fronds for blades. What was I supposed to do? I couldn't cancel, I didn't have any way of contacting him. And it's super rude to tell someone you aren't coming when they show up at your door. I just needed a little push, a hint that I was supposed to go to lunch with this man who was power to the tenth out of my league, and his probably equally sexy friends.

My phone chirped on the bed next to me, and I picked it up. There was only one person who would text me, since just about everyone else in my life had split the second they heard Gavin and I were separated.

BIRDIE:

I can feel you freaking out from here. *Kiss Emoji*

FAITH:

I'm not freaking out. *Frowny Face Emoji*

BIRDIE:

I can almost see you laying on your bed, all your clothes in piles around you, and you are in your bra and panties. And those probably don't match. *Grin Emoji*

FAITH:

No one's going to see my panties to know if they match. *Bikini Emoji*

BIRDIE:

So you're starkers, then. *Smirk Emoji*

FAITH:

I'm not any good at this. I have never really dated. I met Gavin, and six months later we got married. How do I do this?

BIRDIE:

I thought it was just lunch. *Smirk Emoji* *Kiss Emoji* *Heart Emoji*

FAITH:

Frowny Face Emoji *Expletive Emoji* *Heart Emoji*

BIRDIE:

Wear the red bikini I packed you, and the white cover-up. And those sparkly black flip-flops.

FAITH:

That's not real clothes. That bikini barely holds my tits, and the cover-up is see-through. *Wide Eye Emoji*

BIRDIE:

I know. *Wink Emoji* *Kiss Emoji*

FAITH:

I don't need to get laid. I need to heal.

BIRDIE:

You can do both. How much better would it be to heal with a nice gigantic cock in you, making you forget Cheater McCheaterson's face?

FAITH:

He's like eleven degrees of hot. I'm talking
abs for days, tattoos and this dimple on
his cheek that I want to bite.

BIRDIE:

Red bikini, white coverup, black sparkly
flip-flops. *Tiger Emoji*

FAITH:

You are exactly no help. *Eye Roll Emoji*

BIRDIE:

You're welcome. *Kissy Face Emoji*

I tossed the phone down on my bed and grabbed the red bikini. Well, when in Rome, right? It wasn't like I would ever see them again after the trip. Who cared if they thought I was just a little too big to look perfect in a bikini? Who cared if my stomach bunched up more than I would like when I sat down?

Pre-divorce me would have cared. She would have freaked out at the idea of putting on a skimpy red two piece and going out in public. Gavin would have had a meltdown, too. But I was a new person now. I was sans douchebag ex-husband who knocked up his secretary while we were still married. And I didn't give two figs what sexy Cupid thought of my thighs.

I nodded my head once and flipped my hair over my shoulder. I caught a glimpse of my phone, which had a thumbs up emoji from Birdie, then I stalked towards the bathroom.

Vix

I watched Cupid run around the cabin we were sharing, like his backside was on fire.

Correction.

I watched Cupid run around the cabin like his backside was on fire, and there was no snow conveniently everywhere to fix the problem. I suppose that he could also put the ocean to use for such a function. But never mind that, as from my vantage point, it did not look as if his asshole was actually burning.

Our buddy Blitz was a bit of a pyro and had lit all of us on fire at least once at some point or another. Usually without meaning to. He found lighting farts on fire especially entertaining. To say that Cupid had caught his backside on fire more than once would be an understatement.

Today, he merely seemed uncharacteristically panicked.

Cupid didn't panic. He more often than not made an inappropriate pun when faced with stress.

I picked my tablet back up and checked the weather report. Sunny and beautiful. It always was when we came to the resort. Almost like someone made sure of it. Then I flipped back to the mission brief I was trying to memorize before we had to report in on Christmas Eve for final prep. The Team might all think I was a bit of a brown noser, but who did they turn to when things went pear-shaped?

Yeah, me. That's right.

"So, who are we having lunch with again?" I tip the tablet forward against my chin so I can see Cupid exiting his room yet again, in a towel holding two different pairs of swim trunks.

My animal stiffened inside of me when I caught a whiff of something delicious. Cinnamon and vanilla. I wasn't unfamiliar with the scents. I had smelled them many a time together. But this faint hint caused my animal to stir, and the other animal in my shorts to awaken, despite the fact that I was looking at Cupid who was waving swim trunks at me. I love Cupid like a brother, but I had no interest in what he was hiding under that towel.

Side note: I've seen under that towel - which he usually skips - far more often than I would like to admit.

Cupid held up both pairs of trunks. "Which ones?"

"The blue ones," I said without looking, trying instead to identify where that scent was coming from.

"They're both blue, man." Cupid gave me an exasperated and mildly panicked look, which sat oddly on my old friend's face. Cupid was the jovial one. He always had a joke on his tongue, and let any perceived slight roll off his back, like a duck in water. This lunch date was clearly stirring him.

"The bluer blue one, then." I flick my hands at him, done with his shenanigans for the time. I had a mate to find. A mate that needed claiming. That was the scent. My mate.

Cupid dropped both arms to his side and huffed away. "God, you're such an asshole!" The slamming door solidified my concern that something was wrong with Cupid.

"Why is Cupid acting like a sixteen-year-old girl getting ready for her first date?" Dash dropped into the chair next to me, a beer bottle in his hand. I checked my watch, eleven am. Well, it was five o'clock somewhere, I presumed. I shouldn't judge, Dash only ever drank when we were on vacation, unlike some others on our team, who shall remain nameless.

"Apparently we are meeting his friend for lunch and he's in a tizzy because he can't decide which blue pair of swim trunks to wear." I put my tablet down, knowing I wouldn't get any more work done now that Dash was up. I had agreed to "have fun" for the day. This was in exchange for a weekend full of silence from the other two about my study habits.

"Cupid's gone sideways over a girl?" Dash set his bottle down and ran his hands over his face. "Fuck."

"My sentiments exactly."

4

Faith

My fucking suit was riding up my ass when there was a knock at my cabin door. Which didn't bode well for the success of Birdie's outfit of choice. But, it was too late to change. I stopped in front of the mirror by the door to check and make sure my boobs were securely in place under the two little triangles of the suit. Nipples fully covered, I opened the door. Then my mouth dropped to the ground, and I'm sure I was drooling.

Cupid was just as perfect as I remembered. Bare chest glistening in the sun, dark blue board shorts hanging low on his hips, displaying that mouthwatering vee that only the truly dedicated manage to obtain. And let's not forget that dimple. Gleaming white straight teeth peeked out from between his bite-able lips. Sue me, I have a thing for good teeth. Okay, I'm a little weirdly obsessed with nice teeth.

Behind him were two men who clearly worked out just as hard as Cupid did. All glistening muscles and broad shoulders.

I stood there and gawked. Not a word came from my lips. My mouth was dry. And I really wanted to skip lunch and climb all three of them. Right on the little deck in front of my cabin.

What was wrong with me?

"Faith." Cupid's hand on my arm gently pulled me from the doorway until masculine beauty surrounded me. God, I could smell how perfect they were. The scent of masculine musk and salt air mixed with something spicy that reminded me of Christmas morning—that ephemeral essence of Christmas, knowing Santa had come when you were a child, if you could bottle that. Then the three men who stood on my porch had bathed in it.

Cupid drew me under his arm. The feel of his skin sent shivers of arousal down my body, pooling in the bottoms of the red bikini tied precariously around my hips. "These are my buddies. Vix is the one that looks like the stick up his ass is constipating."

"Excuse his crass comment, my dear." Fuck me, he was British. My panties burst into flames. Not that I was wearing any, but whatever. "My friends call me Vix." He took my hand and pulled me from under Cupid's arm. I instantly felt bereft of Cupid's body heat, but enchanted by the gentleman in front of me all at the same time. He brought my knuckles to his lips and pressed a kiss against them. So gently it felt like angel wings against my skin. Or maybe those were the butterflies in my stomach.

"And I'm Dash." The third man pushed Vix out of his way and pulled me into his arms in a hug that ended with a kiss on the cheek. "God, you smell good." He pressed his face into the crook of my neck. Any other time I would have shoved him away for being so forward. But seeing as I wanted to rub myself all over him, I would not complain about some sniffing.

I stood there for far too long just letting Dash hold me. The scent of his skin overtaking all of my senses. "Lunch!" I jumped away from Dash when I realized how weird I was being and glanced over at Cupid, who looked as stunned by my behavior as I was. "We're going to lunch," I finished lamely.

"Well then, my dear." Vix offered me his arm with a winning smile that instantly made my brain melt. I took his arm, only to also find myself pressed against the side of Cupid's body when he threw his arm over my shoulder. "Let us have lunch."

"Hey." Dash pushed Vix away a second time and wrapped his arm around my waist, trapping me in between his body and Cupid's.

I was dead. That was the only explanation. The plane went down over the Caribbean, and this is heaven. And I was being really well rewarded for being a jilted ex.

"Didn't I say there had to be one for all of us?" Dash hugged me closer and I could feel his nose in my hair, inhaling. What shampoo did I use in my morning shower? Cause I was going to have to invest heavily in that company. "I promise, we'll share with you, Vix. You just have to put your tablet down to participate."

"I left my tablet in my room, Dasher," Vix grumbled behind us as we made our way down the beach path.

"Dasher?" I look at the man towering over me. He had a full sleeve of intricate tribal patterns down his right arm, that I was aching to look at - and lick, let's be honest. "Like the reindeer?"

"Very similar." He grinned down at me and squeezed my waist where his hand was holding firm. Gods, his hands were enormous. His fingers reached almost all the way to my belly button, his index finger reaching just inches below my breast, and his pinkie casually brushed my bikini bottoms.

"You have no idea." Cupid winked down at me and steered us down the boardwalk towards the resort's outdoor dining room. "Ain't that right, Dasher?"

"Fuck off, man." Dash took his hand off my hip and pinched Cupid. Hard enough that he let go of me and scowled at his friend. Vix deftly took his place and wrapped his arm around my shoulder.

"They often act like children," he whispered close enough to my ear that the words tickled, and I could breathe in his scent. That ephemeral Christmas had come early essence, mixed with mint, that was probably toothpaste. I wanted to turn my head and lick the taste off his lips. Instead, I rolled my lip into my mouth and bit into it, and nodded. "Please do not let that put you off. I assure you, they are worthy men."

"Shouldn't you be discouraging me from getting attached to them?" I raised a brow.

"But why, my dear?" His fingers grazed my chin, so I looked up directly into his molten brown eyes. "We are not in competition." Right, because I was the stupid girl who got left for the secretary - I'm sorry, administrative assistant - and they were crazy sexy and could have any woman on the beach. "I am confident that there is enough of you to go around."

I had nothing to say to that.

Had he just implied that he and his friends wanted to share me? I searched deep down, but couldn't come up with one reason to argue. I mean, reverse harem romance had always intrigued me. And I was on vacation. Why not have a little fun before I headed back to reality?

Cupid

One mate for the three of us.

Well, the three of us that were there. There were six more guys back at base. But something inside of me told me that none of the others were meant for my Faith. Just Dash, Vix, and me. The thought of Rudy or Don touching my mate made my animal revolt. But Vix or Dash rubbing their hands down her skin, pulling at the nipples I could see pebbled under the flimsy excuse for a coverup? Yeah, that thought made my trunks feel a little too tight.

I needed to get our mate on board, because I needed to claim her. I needed to rub my scent all over her and tell all the other males on the beach that this sexy goddess was ours. You could look, but God help you if you tried to touch; my kind coveted our mates fiercely.

We steered Faith into a horseshoe-shaped booth at the back of the outdoor dining room and I pulled her in after me, so we surrounded her. Dash pouted when Vix beat him to the spot on her other side.

"So." I tucked her under my arm, allowing all four of us to fit into the booth. Faith fit nicely against my side, her body melting against mine. I could see that Vix was taking liberties - as he would say - and had his hand on her thigh. I wished I had thought of that. "What is a sexy woman like you doing all alone on vacation?"

Faith cleared her throat and looked uncomfortable. I instantly wanted to take the question back, but it was already out there in the universe. "Well. . ." She fidgeted under my arm, biting on that tempting bottom lip of hers. "This was supposed to be a surprise trip for my husband and I." I grabbed her left hand, and ran my finger over her bare index finger. She gently pulled her hand from mine and ran her thumb over the inside of the same finger. A nervous habit. From when there was a ring there. "But the same day that the tickets came, he told me he was leaving me."

"Asshole." Dash growled. I could feel his animal expanding inside of him. I looked over and caught his nearly black eyes. Not the dancing green they were usually. "What man would leave someone like you?"

"One that had knocked up his secretary." Faith whispered into her lap. Hurt radiated off her skin. And we needed to fix that fast.

"His loss." Vix nodded to us. "Because now you are free to be ours."

"I don't understand what that means." Faith pulled slightly away from Vix, but his hand tightened around the top of her thigh. "I'm just here on vacation."

I gave Vix a chastising look over Faith's head. Which was usually his job. Fuck. Our mate was messing around with his brain. Dash was nodding along with Vix. What was happening? Since when was I the sensible one? We couldn't scare her off before we solidified the bond.

"He means that you're free to hang out with us," I said through clenched teeth as I tried to get Vix to settle. *You can't claim her here!* I tried to telegraph to Vix, who seemed to realize that it would cause some problems if we stripped our mate bare and had our way with her in the middle of the restaurant.

"Yes," he finally agreed, loosening his hold on her thigh. "You can spend your vacation getting to know us."

"That sounds nice," Faith breathed, then cleared her throat. "I mean, I would like to get to know you, too."

Yeah, get to know her. And then claim her. Because my animal was busting to sink our teeth into our mate and never let go. Instead I leaned in, giving her as much time as possible to move away. And captured that full bottom lip between mine.

Fuck, she tasted like snicker-doodles and heaven. I swept my tongue against the seam of her lips and the groan she let escape made me instantly hard. I needed more. I took her face between my hands and pulled her against my chest; the table prevented me from pulling her all the way into my lap, but just feeling her pressed against me was almost enough. Her hand curled around my neck as she pressed her scantily clad body against me and my animal grunted his approval.

"Oh, my gosh." Faith pulled away abruptly, wiping her chin of her lip gloss that we had smudged, and looked at me wide eyed. "We can't do that here."

"Why not?" I tipped her chin up and nipped at her full lips. "We have great chemis-tree."

"That's just wrong." Dash muttered from his seat beside Vix. "No puns, dude. We're supposed to get her to like us, not turn her off with your lame ass dad jokes. If you're not going to take this seriously, then move over, cause I will."

"He's just jealous that I got to kiss you first." I ran my hand down her shoulder and pulled at the hip farthest from me, making her lean fully into me again. "What do you say, you gonna let us check something off your wish-list tonight?"

"How do you know what's on my list?" She asked, licking my bottom lip and running her hand down my chest. And yep, she's definitely noticed my very obvious boner.

"Because it's the same thing that's on ours." Vix pulled Faith back from me and captured her around the neck, tilting her head back until he could reach her lips. His dominant streak was definitely showing. I bet he was envisioning all the ways our mate would let him tie her up. That had never really been my thing, but suddenly I couldn't wait to watch.

Fuck. She was sexy. And the more aroused she got, the better she smelled. I watched her kiss Vix while she touched me. Her fingers ghosted down my chest before she hooked her hands into the top of my trunks, pulling me into her body. I wanted nothing more than to lick the salt air off of her skin. I wanted to pull those taut nipples into my mouth, taste her flavor. But the waitress completely ruined the moment by clearing her throat.

"I'm sorry to interrupt." No, she wasn't. The sarcasm in her tone just oozed jealousy and gave her a sour, foul smell. I smirked at her and pulled away from Faith, who looked more than a little uncomfortable at being caught making out with three guys. Well, two. Dash was scowling on his side of the booth. We'd fix that later. "But you can't do that here. If you're not going to order, I suggest you take your little party elsewhere."

"My apologies." Vix straightened Faith's coverup, where it had ridden up over her thighs, and swept his thumb under his bottom lip to rid himself of the last of the cherry-colored gloss that painted his face. "We would love to have some menus."

"Right." The waitress rolled her eyes and turned on a heel to leave.

5

Dash

We spent the day together, getting to know each other, and getting a little more comfortable touching. Explaining to Faith that we were a packaged deal took a little convincing, but in the end she relented. She still thought we just meant for the remainder of our vacations, but we would straighten that out before we left for good just after New Years'. Humans didn't feel the mating pull the same way that shifters did, but we could all tell that Faith was feeling something.

Gods, just getting to touch my mate's skin was heaven. But not getting any further was its own special hell. At dinner, somehow we got the same cranky waitress, who gave us all disdainful looks. One particularly scathing one at Faith as she sat across my lap, letting me feed her bites of the surf and turf we ordered. Faith gave her a squinty look as soon as our waitress turned her back.

"She's mean." Faith glared daggers at her, then opened wide for me to place a bite of perfectly cooked steak on her tongue.

"She's just jealous," Cupid said with his mouth full of his own grilled veggie dinner. It smelled amazing, but I needed meat. His argument for being a vegetarian was that our animals weren't predators. My argument was that meat was delicious.

"Whatever her problem is, I'd rather she not be our waitress again." Faith re-situated herself in my lap and had to feel my dick grinding against her cheeks as she did so. "I'm done." She patted her stomach as her head lulled against my shoulder, her cheeks flushed from the alcohol in the mojitos she had been downing like water. For all that, we were at a resort, and they were probably more club soda than rum, our beautiful mate had probably drunk about half a dozen. Which meant that our little Faith was completely schnockered.

"I'm gonna see you home then, love." I helped her to her feet and watched as she pressed her lips to both Cupid and Vix's in turn. Both of which were careful not to let the kiss go too far. After all, she was so drunk that I was half convinced that my arm was the only thing keeping her from slowly tipping to one side. Also, we all held to the same code. Faith turned back to me and stumbled against my chest.

"Let's go, big boy." She gave me a crooked grin and patted my chest. "I guess you're the lucky one tonight, eh?" She wiggled her eyebrows at me, then managed to trip over nothing. The only thing keeping her off the floor was my grip on her waist.

"I'm going to get you to bed."

"Yeah, you are." She wiggled her brows at me again and nearly collided with our server, who had a tray loaded down with glasses. I swear the woman growled as I swept Faith past her.

"I'm going to make sure you drink water and then I'll see you tomorrow." I steered her around tables and people as she gaped up at me. "You're drunk."

"I'm not that drunk." She snuggled into my chest. "Will you at least stay with me?" Faith asked so quietly I would have missed it if I were human. "Please?" She looked up at me under hooded eyes, and I could feel the vulnerability flowing off her in waves. "I don't want to be alone."

"Yeah." I nodded down to her, a sick feeling growing in my stomach. That husband of hers must have really done a number on her. "Of course I'll stay." That unworthy look in her eyes needed to be addressed quickly. I pressed a kiss to her cheek and hugged her tightly.

"I've just been so lonely." Her arms banded around my waist as she let me guide her back to her cabin. "Not just since Gavin left. I mean, I should have seen the signs long before he left." Faith halted in the middle of the path and looked off into nothing. "I mean, how many meetings can someone have that go til after ten? How often do you go to the gym at midnight, and then not come home before work?" She turned and looked at me, her eyes distant. "I'm a complete idiot."

"You're not an idiot." I cupped her cheeks and looked down into her glistening eyes. Tears threatened to overflow. Then she blinked. In the moonlight they glimmered on her lashes like diamonds. I carefully rubbed them off her cheeks with my thumbs and looked down into her eyes. "He is, for letting you go."

"You're just being nice 'cause you want to get into my pants." Faith pulled away from me and stumbled a few steps down the path. "You don't have to walk me home, Dash." She waved over her shoulder, clearly meant to dismiss me. "I can take it from here."

"Faith." I called after her as she kept walking. "I'm not trying to get into your pants."

"Liar," she practically spat at me. Oh, I could feel the venom in her voice. The alcohol had taken a turn from vulnerable to angry and hurt.

"Okay, fair point." I sighed and ran my hands through my hair before jogging to catch up to her. "I can't think of anything more pleasurable than making love to you. But that's not happening tonight. I've already told you that."

"Men say that so it seems like it was the woman's idea to seduce them." Faith stumbled, huffed, and then kicked her sandals off. They disappeared into the foliage that lined the path. I made note of where we were so I could find them in the morning. Fuck, she was cute drunk. Frustrating and a little emotional, but cute. "I'm not falling for that again."

She certainly was not. She was mine. Mine. . . and Vix and Cupid's. And we would never manipulate her like that. "Please, just let me get you home and get some water in you. You drank kind of a lot today. And with all the sun."

"No sex." She pointed at me, scrunching up her face, trying desperately to look serious. But she just looked drunk... and a little green around the edges. I just held my hands out in surrender. "I mean it mister, you are not getting into my swimsuit bottoms."

"I just want to get you home safe."

"Dash?" Faith's face crumpled. "I don't feel so good." Her face paled, and she grabbed for my arm before bending over and emptying the contents of her stomach all over the front of my swim trunks.

Faith

The sun felt like it was inside my bedroom. I was hot and achy and it was far too bright. I rubbed my face and turned away from the light, firmly pressing my face into something hard and warm. "What the hell?" I grumbled, pushing against the body in my bed. Something was wrong.

"I was wondering if you were ever going to wake up." I blinked up at the man sitting up against the headboard of my bed, my Kindle in his hand. "So, shifter romance, huh?"

"What are you doing here?" I rubbed the drool off my face, and considered wiping it off Cupid's thigh, too. But he was a big boy and could do that himself.

"Dash called last night after you puked on him." Cupid shrugged and went back to reading. "Bear shifters, really? Kinda played out, don't you think? I mean, half the paranormal romance authors out there have a bear book.

It's all about the predator shifters, too." I could almost hear him rolling his eyes as he clicked his tongue in exaggerated annoyance. But he hadn't answered my question. Not really.

"I like bears," I said, sitting up and looking down at myself. I was in a tiny pair of sleep shorts and a white tank top that did not hide my nipples from the entire room. And boy, were they perky. I might have felt like shit steaming in the tropical sun after being run over by an eighteen wheeler, but my nipples were oh so very ready to play. "Did you dress me?"

"Nope." Cupid just grinned, and my stomach plummeted.

"We didn't have sex, did we?" I whispered, not meeting his eyes. "Oh God."

"Would it have been so bad?" he actually sounded a little offended. "I mean, I'm a pretty decent looking guy, and you seemed to like me just fine yesterday."

"No." I shook my head, and then instantly regretted it when white hot pain swam around my brain and my stomach rolled dangerously. "I mean. I don't remember last night."

"No, we didn't have sex." Cupid turned off the tablet and put it down on the nightstand. "You threw up on Dash, he called us from your cabin and asked for a change of clothes. When we got here, you were stripping and trying to climb him, after he had put you both fully clothed into the shower." Oh, God. I dropped my face into my hands and waited for the ground to open up and eat me. "He disentangled himself and left you with me and went to change. When I convinced you to get out of the shower, you danced your way into the bedroom and fell asleep naked and wet on the bed. It took all three of us to wrestle you into your sleep wear while you kicked and sang Christmas songs at the top of your lungs."

"Oh, my God." I wanted to die right then. "Why are you still here?" I muttered into my hands. "I mean, you could have just left me."

"Well, you're like an octopus when you sleep, and you managed—in your sleep, mind you—to entangle Vix into your surprisingly powerful embrace. So we stayed." Cupid shrugged like it was no big deal, but I was beyond mortified.

Vix chose that moment to appear out of the kitchen, two mugs of coffee in his hands. "Oh, wonderful, you have finally awakened." He put the coffee mugs on the bedside table and disappeared again. "I have a bottle of water and some acetaminophen for your head." He came back through the door and dropped two white tablets into my hand before cracking open the top of a water bottle and handing it to me. "Down you go." He made a hurry up gesture. "You have to admit that you'll feel a great deal better once you've taken your pills." I looked at the pills in my hand. Definitely Tylenol, not that I think he would roofie me or anything. They all had ample opportunity while I was drunk and throwing myself at them. I tossed the medicine back and chased it with a healthy gulp of water. I went to hand the bottle back to Vix, but he shook his head. "Drink the entire bottle, please. Then you can have coffee."

"I'm back." The front door to my cabin banged closed, and I could hear the jingle of keys hitting the table. "Is our mate up yet? I got her a couple of breakfast burritos." The rustling of paper bags followed. "Britany? The waitress who hates us? Yeah, I'm pretty sure it's just Faith she doesn't like. She slipped me her number. I tried to tell her I was taken, but she just winked and said for after Christmas, whatever that means."

"Faith's up," I called out and then growled and held my head while it splintered into pieces. "What do you mean 'mate?' And what about after Christmas?"

"Oh hey, you're up." Dash handed me the bag of greasy breakfast. He looked over at the other two men. They both just shook their heads. "I guess we have some explaining to do."

6

Vix

"So." Dash sat down in the armchair and scooted it to face the bed. He leaned forward on his knees and ran his hands over his face. "There's some stuff we should probably tell you about."

"About the 'mate' thing? Yeah, I'd like you to explain that." Faith dropped the bag of breakfast on the bed and folded her arms across her chest. "I mean, I'm down for a little fun on vacation, but that's all. I just fucking got divorced, and mate seems to be a bit of a long-term thing."

"While that would usually be true for us as well, this is a little different." I gingerly sat on the corner of the bed and wiped my suddenly very sweaty palms on my jeans. "Our kind, once they find their perfect match, mates for life. The three of us were becoming concerned that we had not met our match as of yet. But it seems that we just weren't looking in the right places."

"Go back." Faith shook her head and pushed away from Cupid, sitting up on her knees on the bed and glaring at all of us in turn. "Your *kind*? Is this some creepy religious thing, cause I am not interested if that's the case. I don't need some guys coming in and trying to indoctrinate me into a cult while I'm still vulnerable." Her eyes bore into me like I had personally offended her. "If you think you can sucker me into something, you are so very wrong. And you can leave." She pointed to the door, going as far as to push on Cupid, who didn't budge. "I said get out."

"Please." I stood and helped Cupid off the bed. The look of hurt that marred my good friend's face tugged harder on my heart than usual. "Give us just five minutes to explain, then if you want us to leave, we will."

Faith just looked at me. She didn't need words. Her face told me everything. We had five minutes and then we might lose our mate forever. I looked over to Dash and then at Cupid. They both shrugged their shoulders, and Dash hooked his thumbs into the waistband of his swim trunks and began rolling them down his hips.

"What the actual fuck do you think you're doing?" Faith screeched so loudly that I was sure it was making her already aching head explode with pain. She covered her face with her hands. "Put your fucking clothes back on."

"This is a show and tell kinda thing, darling." Dash dropped his shorts on the floor and kicked out of them. "It's gonna defeat the purpose if you don't look."

"Put your pants back on and I'll look." She growled as she squeezed her eyes shut and held her head. "Please."

"You promised five minutes."

"I didn't think you would wave your dick at me during that time," she countered.

"Fair point." Dash consented and looked at me. I had nothing. In my entire life, I had never met a tactical situation that I couldn't think my way out of. There was always an answer. But faced with trying to explain what we were to our mate in a way she would believe without visuals? I was at a loss.

"Faith, if you would indulge us for just a moment. I promise that Dash is not trying to persuade you through sex." I carefully crawled onto the bed and touched her cheeks, pulling her hands away from her head until she looked at me. "If I were to simply tell you that Cupid, Dash, and I weren't human, would you believe me?"

"Not a fucking chance."

"Then please allow us to demonstrate." I nodded to Dash. My friend hunched down and let his body shatter before it reformed into his other skin. The hooves of his animal clacked on the floor, and he had to duck his head just a bit to keep his antlers from catching in the chandelier. "We are reindeer shifters and our kind, once we meet our mate, mates for life."

"I don't know what to say." Faith's mouth hung open as she openly stared at Dash. Our form was larger than the average reindeer, and he took up nearly all the extra space in the cabin's bedroom. He carefully bent his front legs and lay down on the floor, so he could hold his head up all the way. "That was just Tylenol, right?"

"Yes, of course." I nodded, rubbing my hand up and down her back. She slumped back into me, allowing me to hold her in my arms. Something deep and bright settled inside of me as she lay her head against my shoulder, still staring at Dash in wonder. "We aren't a large community, but there are several different species of shifter."

"And the books I read?"

"Probably written by shifters." Cupid sat back down on the bed. "At least the one you've been reading. Cause it gets a bunch of stuff right."

"So. . ." Faith couldn't seem to take her eyes off of Dash, who looked back at us before changing back into his two-legged form. "When we bumped into each other yesterday?" She finally pulled her eyes from Dash as he pulled his trunks back on. "You knew."

"The second you touched me, I knew you were mine." Cupid confirmed. "I wanted to introduce you to my friends, I wanted to show off my mate."

"But you didn't know. . ."

"That you were their mate, too? Nope." Cupid took her hand, and she let him pull her across the bed to him. He curled his arms around her and rubbed his face against hers. Leaving traces of his scent on her skin. "I mean, it happens, but not often."

"What does this all mean for me?" Faith sagged against Cupid like her strings had been cut. I imagine that it was a lot to take in while suffering from a hangover, and without coffee.

"For now, it means you get to know us." Dash dropped back down in the armchair he had been sitting in. "You'll probably feel more drawn to us than you would a normal guy, but you don't have to do anything you don't want. Just give us a chance."

"Okay." She nodded and tucked herself back under the covers, pulling Cupid with her. "Can we go back to bed and start this day over in an hour or so?"

"Sure thing, sweetheart." Cupid dropped a kiss to the top of her head. "You want us to stay or go?"

"Stay?" She looked over at me and held out her hand. "I want some sober snuggles that I will actually remember. Then we're gonna start this day over properly. With coffee. And scones. Little ones that have gooey icing."

"Sounds heavenly." I tuck myself against her front as Cupid spoons into her back. Dash just sighs and punches his pillow before settling in behind me.

"Next time I get the cuddles."

"You practically got a lap dance in the shower." Faith mumbled against my chest. "Shut up and go to sleep."

"Yes, ma'am."

7

Faith

I woke up far too warm, pushing away the covers and trying to wriggle out from between Cupid and Vix, who had me caged in down on the bed. Vix was practically laying on top of me, his very obvious morning wood pressed into my hip in a way that I couldn't imagine was comfortable. I shoved at his chest until he opened his eyes and pinned me to the bed in a whole new way.

"Is that a candy cane in your pocket, or are you just happy to see me?" I reached up to cup his cheek, needing to touch him.

"Faith." His voice was gravely from sleep and ran like liquid fire all the way down to my core. I rolled my hips up against the ridge of his erection, and that seemed to bring him back to the present. "I do apologize."

"No apology needed." My fingers sank into his hair as I pulled him back down to me. "Just making sure it was for me." I ran my tongue across the seam of his lips and grinned into the kiss as he took over, biting and pulling at my bottom lip as he rolled his hips down against me, making me burn.

"Always for you, my dear." Vix slid his hands over my hips and pulled me tightly against him. "Good morning." He smiled against my lips and pulled me back into a fierce kiss. "I have been waiting forever to have you."

"I want to remind you we're still here." Dash appeared over Vix's back, his hair sleep tousled and his eyes still heavy. "I mean, by all means, carry on. But don't forget Cupid and I are watching."

"And possibly participating." Cupid pushed Vix's head out of the way and captured my lips himself. "Hey beautiful."

"Morning, babe." I smiled up at my goofy Dash. My mate with the dancing green eyes.

Fuck. My mate. This was fast right? I mean in all those shifter romances that's how it happened. Bam. And then you have this perfect someone forever. God, what had I gotten myself into. But then I looked over at Dash, and his bite-able abs, and his perfectly lush lips. I had this fire inside of me, and looking at him - at any of them - just stoked it higher. The butterflies in my belly were dragons, and it all felt so right.

"Um. . . So, how does this work?" I struggled to pull my eyes from the dips and valleys of Dash's washboard stomach to look at all of them.

I took in each of the men in my bed. Vix on his knees between my legs, his shorts tented quite obviously. Cupid still snuggled under the covers at my side, his nose nuzzling mine as he hummed happily to himself. And finally Dash, my left out baby. Always feeling pushed aside by his friends. No wonder drunk me had tried to climb him. Not only was he devastatingly sexy with his dark green eyes and his jet black hair, but he had this aura of need that surrounded him.

"How do you want it to work?" Dash held me with his gaze, the intensity ramping up the heat that I had been feeling before he interrupted Vix.

"I want you," I whispered, reaching out my hand to him. He took it gently in his own and kissed my knuckles. "I want you to touch me, Dash." Vix started to move away, but I stopped him with my legs wrapped around his hips. "I want you *all* to touch me."

"How about we start with coffee and take a beat?" Vix petted me softly on my thigh, his thumb disappearing just a little bit under my sleep shorts, inches from where I wanted it, where I needed him to touch me.

"Is this the bond?" I asked as I lifted my hips, trying to chase his fingers. "Is that why I'm so fucking horny?"

"Partially." Cupid rubbed his face against mine, just our cheeks brushing, and it felt sinfully good. I just wanted to rub myself all over him. "It might be a little because you woke up with three hot guys in your bed."

Vix pulled his hands away from where I was still trying to get them under my shorts and pulled at my ankles until I let go of his hips. "The bond can feel very strong at the beginning. Especially with three mates." He pulled Cupid up by his shoulders and herded both he and Dash off the bed. "It is our job to be responsible with the hormones you're experiencing and not allow any of us to do something we regret."

"I won't regret it." I kick the rest of the covers away and hook my fingers into the waistband of my sleep shorts. "Promise." I pushed the shorts down and reached for the guys.

"Faith." Vix carefully pulled the covers back over me and took my hand. "My love. Please, will you let us take this all a little at a time?"

"I want you," I pouted.

"And I can think of nothing I would rather do than sink into your wet heat and lose myself." He cupped my cheeks gently in his hands and took my lips carefully, reverently with his. "But we must remember ourselves. Let me buy you breakfast."

"Okay." I pulled his lips back to mine, and he allowed me to lick slowly into his mouth, exploring every crevice with loving touches. "But I want sexy times tonight."

"I think we can agree to that."

Cupid

Sitting on the beach listening to Vix tell Faith stories about what a fuck up I was when I was younger was not exactly my idea of a good time, but with Faith snuggled up in my towel with me, I would put up with it. That is until I see a familiar face that shouldn't be in the Caribbean at all.

"Hate to interrupt, Vix." I nod my chin to where I saw Krampus. What the fuck was he doing there? "You think we should say something?"

"I find myself not really caring." Vix sat down on his own towel and picked up his beer, which had to be a little warm; he had been talking for quite some time. "I'll let the general know, but we have better things to do."

"What's wrong?" Faith twisted around in my lap, trying to see what we were all looking at.

"Nothing, just Sourpuss." Dash took a long pull from his beer and shook his head. "Don't worry about it."

It made something in my stomach turn to see Krampus at our resort. He stood in a group of women. Some girl, that definitely had more boobs than brains, was plastered against his chest, stroking that nasty black goatee that dripped from his chin like offal. I wrapped my arms tighter around Faith and breathed in her scent. I took one last look over the top of Faith's head, my nose buried in her hair, and locked eyes with the bearded man. He gave me a grotesque sneer and then went back to his bimbos.

"We should make our way back to the cabin," I said after a long moment of taking in the comfort of having my mate in my arms. "Clean up for dinner. Didn't you want to go see the tree lighting tonight?" I nuzzled against the crook of her neck. I did not want to go to the tree lighting, I wanted to get my mate nice and naked, and spend the night getting her off.

"It would be nice. We don't have to." She shrugged and looked at the other guys. "We don't just have to do what I want. We can do whatever you all want too."

"Oh, we will." Dash winked at her. "But we can go see the lights before I eat your pussy."

"Dash!"

"What? No one's listening." He dropped to his knees next to us and leaned in close so he could whisper into Faith's ear. "I wanna fuck you like an animal. I want to watch as Vix and Cupid make you cum over and over."

Faith arched back against me, pressing her perfectly round ass against my burgeoning erection. "Please." Her voice came out husky and breathy. And yep, we were done with the beach. I stood and swung her over my shoulder and headed towards the cabins.

"Cupid, put me down." she wiggled against my shoulder, but I held her tight. I felt Dash lay a smack against her upturned bottom, and couldn't help but laugh as she squealed. The scent of her arousal perfumed the surrounding air, as Dash smacked the other cheek. "Fuck," she growled and sagged over my shoulder. "I need you." Faith grabbed at my ass through my trunks, kneading my flesh as her arousal deepened. We were off the beach and up the path to her cabin before she slid her hands down the back of my shorts, her little fingers burning a trail over my skin.

Dash opened the cabin door for us, and I strode directly into her bedroom, dropping her down on the bed and pulled the ties for her bikini bottoms before she even stopped bouncing. Her thighs fell open for me and my world narrowed down to that strip of dripping wet flesh. "God you're perfect." I was wrenched to my knees with the need to rub my face in her scent. "You smell so good." She went stiff under my tongue as I rolled it over her slit and circled around her clit. "Get that top off, gorgeous. We feast tonight." I gave the top of her slit a gentle kiss and shucked my trunks. "And we have some nice big presents for you, mate." I could hear the others dropping their shorts and climbing onto the bed surrounding Faith.

"We're gonna be cumming down your chimney tonight," Dash growled as his trunks hit the floor and he kicked them away. The gasp that came from Faith's lips went straight to my dick. Dash tumbled onto the bed next to our mate and captured her lips, digging his fingers into her hair, holding her still as he fucked her mouth with his tongue. Her moans filled the room.

"Oh, baby." I dropped back to my knees between her thighs and ran a finger through her arousal, gathering it and rubbing it up over her clit. Her hips thrust up to meet my fingers as her thighs trembled. "You're on the naughty list this year." My tongue followed the path my fingers had taken, and I had to hold her hips down to continue to delve between her lips. I used the tip of my tongue to tease her opening before thrusting in and fucking her with it. I rolled my eyes up to meet hers and grinned. Vix had finally joined us, his trunks gone. He had her breasts in his hands, as he alternated sucking on one nipple before moving onto the other.

"You are beautiful, Faith," Vix said reverently.

Faith

I was in heaven. Dash's lips were fused to mine as his tongue tangled with my own. The thrust of it between my lips mimicked what Cupid was doing between my thighs, and I was quickly spiraling up to an epic orgasm. When Vix pulled my nipple into his mouth and bit at the distended tip, I was gone. My lips ripped away from Dash's as I howled my release to the room. My legs locked around Cupid's head as I thrust my hips and rode his tongue.

Fuck.

I fell back to the world and grabbed at Dash. "I wanna lick your candy cane, baby." I pulled at his hips until he straddled my face and held onto the headboard above us.

"You sure?" His pupils were completely blown as he looked down at me. I couldn't even see the ring of green that usually looked out at me.

"Fuck yes," I groaned as I felt the tip of Cupid's cock teasing my opening. "I want that cane down my throat while Cupid fucks me." I wrapped my fingers around the base of his dick and licked the bead of pre-cum that spilled from the tip. "Mmm." I rolled my tongue around the head and pulled him between my lips.

"Faith," His hips jerked as I scraped gently at the underside of his shaft and I couldn't help but grin around him. "Do that again."

I was lost. Cupid pressed his way into me, and the stretch of his cock inside me made me groan. I rolled my eyes up to watch Dash as he tentatively started to thrust between my lips. I hummed around him and pulled at his ass cheeks, encouraging him to thrust deeper. The feeling of him at the back of my throat and Cupid thrusting against my g-spot made me want to cry. I relaxed my throat and pulled Dash deeper, his groan the best reward I could think of. My nails made little half moon crescents in the skin of his hips.

"Fuck, you feel good." Cupid's hips pistoned into me, his fingers teasing my clit as he rubbed along that perfect spot inside of me, and my second orgasm snuck up on me. I shattered around him, sucking Dash's cock into my mouth until I felt my nose touch the neatly trimmed pubic hair over his cock.

"Faith, I'm gonna cum." Dash tried to pull away, but I grabbed his ass and kept him where I wanted him. His cock throbbed between my lips, and I felt the warmth of his release pulsing down my throat. "Baby," he sighed as I let him tumble to the bed at my side. "That was everything." He kissed my swollen lips, tasting his own release on my tongue.

"So good." Cupid kissed along my belly as his softening cock fell from inside of me. "Vix has been patient, though."

That made me sit up. And there was Vix, completely naked on the wing chair in my room. His legs were splayed, and he treated me to the sight of his thick shaft, as he languidly stroked himself from root to tip. "You gonna come give me that North Pole?"

"Oh, my dear." Vix stood and I couldn't take my eyes off him as he stalked me across the room. "I'm going to ride you like a reindeer." He prowled over the mattress and struck, crushing our lips together and, just like that, I was ready to go again. Arousal dripped between my legs as he pulled on my hip. "Up on all fours, princess," he growled against my mouth. I let him position me the way he liked, pressing my face back into the mattress next to Dasher, who rubbed up and down my back as Vix pushed his face between my upturned cheeks and licked me from clit to the tight pucker of my asshole. I shivered and squealed as he did it again, but by the third time I relaxed into his hands as they needed my ass cheeks. "When we get home, I want to truss you up with rope, and have my way with you," he growled against my nether lips, and I felt the vibrations of it all the way through my body. "But for now, you have to promise not to move."

"Please," I tried to thrust my hips back into him, but he just laid a sharp smack against my ass. "Vix," I whined, which earned me another smack.

"Oh, you're going to resist, are you, princess?" He bit into the fullness of my cheek and then soothed the skin with his tongue. "I can have Dash hold you down." I groaned and pressed my hips back into him, feeling his thick shaft rub along my crack. "Is that a yes?"

"Please, Vix." I turned my head to look at him and got another sharp hand on my cheeks. I could feel them burn against his palm as he soothed the pain away. "Fuck me, please." My arousal was all but dripping onto the bed below us.

"Oh, I plan on it." He used one hand to press against my shoulders, pushing me down to the bed as he pulled my hips higher and teased my clit with his cock. "Dash, would you be a dear and hold her down?"

"My pleasure," Dash's voice caressed my skin before his hand replaced Vix's. "He's going to make you feel so good, baby." He pressed a kiss to my lips and lay down next to me. His hand stayed firm on my shoulders as Vix gripped my hips.

Vix didn't bother with any teasing. As soon as he had me positioned the way he wanted, he thrust his cock into me in one swift motion. I groaned and tried to wiggle under him as the head of his dick pressed against my cervix, but after a moment of futile movement, I lay still. The feel of him was different from Cupid, who was definitely thicker. Vix pushed so hard at the end of me that for a moment it was uncomfortable before the heavy weight of pleasure flooded my body. "Good girl." His grip loosened on my hip as he started to thrust shallowly, keeping the head of him bumping against my cervix with each thrust. "I can feel you fluttering around me, princess." He leaned down a bit into my shoulder, hard enough that I knew it would bruise. "Do you like that?" He gave me a sharp thrust, then pulled almost all the way out, rolling the head of himself just inside of me.

"No," I whined, trying to push back and take more of him back inside of me. A sharp spank on my ass made me stop moving. "Please, Vix. I want more."

"I will give you everything." He slowly pressed back into me. My thighs trembled as he built up the pleasure between us. Dash kept his hand on my shoulders and licked at my lips as he watched me. "There is so much we can discover together." His hips stuttered, and he held still for a moment. "Let her go," he told Dash, who immediately lifted his hand from my back. "I will show you all the ways your body can find pleasure." Vix wrapped my hair around his hand and pulled me up onto my knees with his cock still deep inside of me, arching my back so he could kiss me as he lazily fucked me. "Mmm, you taste like heaven."

"Vix, please make me cum."

"You haven't had enough pleasure from my brothers?" he asked, slowly thrusting in and out of me with long strokes. "Do you need another orgasm, my beauty?"

"Yes." The burn of my scalp melded with the pressure building in my core as he rubbed along my g-spot, stretching me from a new angle. "Please."

"All in good time." His free hand came down to smack my clit and fire erupted in my body. I tried to curl forward, but his hand in my hair prevented me from moving away. "You will take what I give you." He pinched my throbbing clit between his fingers and pulled. "Do you like that?"

"Yes." He pinched harder and my mind started to white out as he thrust harder into me. "Vix." His cock and fingers worked at me until I melted into him. Little trembles started in my thighs and moved inward until I was convulsing so hard around him that it felt like they filled my entire body with stars. It was so much pleasure that I couldn't contain it, and a scream erupted from my lips as he buried his cock as deep as he could go, and painted my insides with his release.

"Oh, my princess." He gently laid us down on the bed next to Dash. Vix petted my skin as I continued to tremble around him. "You are a marvel." He kissed along my shoulders. "Our perfect marvel."

Dash grinned at me, and I wrapped my arms around him as I trembled between them, Vix's dick still hard and deep inside me. "You are so beautiful." Dash kissed my lips and hooked one of my legs over his hip. My eyes felt so heavy. I wanted to tell them how amazing I felt, how much I enjoyed them, but the words felt like lead on my tongue, and I couldn't keep my eyes open any longer.

"We came, we fucked, we conquered." I heard Cupid say as the bed bounced under me. And then nothing.

8

Vix

I had never really taken the time to look at the resort's decorations around Christmas time. Perhaps I was simply jaded when it came to Christmas, but I preferred to think that Faith was simply opening my eyes to new experiences. That is after all what having a mate was for, to broaden your horizons and to be the yin to my yang as it were. What did I learn with my newly-opened eyes? That palm trees should never be wrapped in lights for any holiday. And most certainly not for Christmas.

"I can't breathe," Cupid gasped out as he doubled over, holding his stomach with both hands. His face was bright red, and he had arrived at that stage of laughter where you were laughing so hard that noise ceased to come out. "Fuck!"

Faith was faring little better as she alternated patting Cupid on his foot and rolled around in the sand holding her own stomach and trying to suck in air faster, then she laughed it out. "Stop!" she gasped and then lay prostrate on the ground at our feet. "Oh, God." She looked up at the lights and immediately started giggling uncontrollably again. "Vix." She held out a hand to me, waving it around until I caught it. "You're gonna have to carry me home."

What did palm trees look like when they were wrapped in Christmas lights? Dicks. They looked like giant dicks. And when you added in the palm fronds? They looked like giant dicks exploding in orgasm. And my mate, and her other mate, had the subsequent maturity of five-year-old boys.

Dash had resorted to sitting on a bench nearby, holding his head in his hands, and occasionally letting out a chuckle.

"If I carry you, who will get Cupid back to your cabin?" I asked as I hauled my boneless mate to her feet and up over my shoulder. "While I'm not completely against leaving him here, I won't hear the end of it if we do."

Faith waved her hands around for a minute and started giggling again. "Dash'll get him," she managed to get out between bouts of laughter. "Dash, come carry Cupid home."

"If I look up, I'll see the penis lights again," Dash called from his bench, his head still in his hands.

"So, your solution is to simply not look at them until they turn the lights out?" I asked as I hefted Faith more comfortably over my shoulder, making sure that her coverup was completely covering her backside as I did.

"I thought it was a solid plan." Dash didn't move to get Cupid, who had fallen completely to the sand and was twitching every once in a while.

"You both can sleep out in the walkway then." I smacked Faith on her round hindquarters and about faced toward where her cabin was located. "I shall simply have to entertain our mate all on my own."

"I'm good!" Cupid bounced to his feet. "We're all good here."

"I thought that would help." I grinned to myself and continued to rub soothing circles on Faith's reddened ass. "Dash? Have you recovered?"

"Can you just lead me back to the cabin?" He stood holding one hand over his eyes and the other waving in front of himself, searching, presumably for one of us. "I'll just keep my eyes closed, and then we'll go back to the cabin and cuddle."

"Just cuddle?" Faith used her hands on my waist to sit up enough to see both of the other men. "But sexy times?" I could hear the pout in her voice. I could also hear the three tequila sunrises that she had ingested at dinner.

"You're drunk." I patted her gently. "Remember what we agreed on."

"Sober sisters." She smacked my ass hard and kicked her legs from where they were draped over my shoulder, nearly flinging one of her flip-flops off into my face. "Giddy up, Vix. The faster we get home, the faster I can be sober."

"I am quite sure that isn't how it works." I mumbled and looked over to where Cupid was humoring Dash and leading him in a mostly straight path towards where Faith's cabin sat on the beach. "But I would like to get some water into you."

"That's what she said." Faith snorted and kicked her legs again. "Let's go."

"I would like to point out that I am also not a horse," I told her as I followed my brethren to the cabin.

"You got hooves, right?"

"Occasionally," I agreed.

She pushed up against my back again and tried to look around. I held my arms firm around her, so she didn't accidentally drop herself on her head with her movement. "So, don't reindeer giddy up, too?"

"Not exactly."

"I wonder what Santa says to his reindeer to make them giddy up?" She dropped herself back down and amused herself with pulling the backs of my swim trunks away from my body and trying to see my ass. It was dark enough that I was mostly sure she wasn't succeeding, not that it would have been a problem. She had seen all of me only hours before.

"I'm led to believe that he uses the words 'On Dasher, on Dancer, on Donner and Vixen. . .' and so forth." I gave a brief smile when she was silent for a long moment. "Faith?" A loud snore answered me, and I carefully maneuvered her into my arms. She curled into my body as I carried her princess style through the door of her cabin, mindful not to bump her head as we proceeded. Cupid and Dash were already sound asleep on the bed. They were under the covers, but I was quite certain that the swim trunks thrown over the wing-backed chair were the ones they had been wearing to dinner.

I lay Faith next to Cupid, and watched as she rolled into him, throwing a leg over his hips and tucking her chin under his. I dropped my trunks over the ones already on the chair and climbed in bed behind her. I looked over at my Faith and her two other mates, and my mind went quiet. I was where I was always meant to be.

Faith

The boys left the day before Christmas. They told me they were going to, but waking up alone with a trio of candy canes and a note made me feel hollow anyhow.

Dash had booked me a snorkel tour of the reef for the morning, so I wouldn't feel lonely, and I would actually leave the cabin. But as I was getting changed for the outing, I kept looking back at our bed. The bed we had spent countless hours in together, and I would return to alone on Christmas Eve night.

I heaved a long sigh, letting my shoulders drop as I turned to grab my keys and head to the beach shed where the tour would start. I could do this. I had gone on the vacation alone. I had never dreamed of meeting anyone while trying to enjoy my second honeymoon without my cheating husband, who didn't want me. There was no reason for me to be melancholy.

Except I was.

I missed my mates and they had only been gone a few hours. How the hell was I supposed to get on with my life back home knowing what it was like to be with them? How was I going to pick up the pieces again?

BIRDIE:

Stop feeling sorry for yourself and get
your ass in gear. *Kissy Face Emoji* *Heart
Emoji*

FAITH:

They left. *Tear emoji*

BIRDIE:

They'll be back. P.S. that tear looks like
spooge. Just saying. *Heart Emoji* *Kiss
Emoji*

FAITH:

Yeah, to the island, but what happens
when I go home?

BIRDIE:

The world works in mysterious ways, my
friend. Have some faith, Faith. *Hug Emoji*

FAITH:

My faith is a little broken right now.
Broken Heart Emoji

BIRDIE:

I know, love. But I promise it won't be
forever. Now go snorkeling. Cupid said he
wanted pictures, right?

FAITH:

Right.

I snagged the underwater disposable camera that Cupid had bought me at the resort gift shop for exactly that reason and walked out the door. It was strange walking the path to the beach alone after having the guys with me every day, but I wrapped the wrist strap of the camera around my hand and tucked my keys into the pocket of my beach cover up and off I went.

The equipment shed where the snorkeling group met was only a few minutes walk from my cabin, but along the way I kept seeing groups and couples chatting and laughing. Was it stupid that I missed the guys? It was just a vacation fling. Just because they promised to come back after whatever mission they had to go on, didn't mean they would. We'd exchanged phone numbers, and other personal fluff that people shared when they were close. But the way they talked about their jobs scared me a little.

I turned off the path and onto the beach proper, shielding my eyes from the sun that crept in over my sunglasses, searching for anyone else who might join me for snorkeling. To my surprise, there was actually quite a group. Most of them seemed to be families and couples, except for one man. Something about the way he watched me as I made my way over to the shed tickled something in the back of my mind. He looked like a classic Disney villain, all the way down to his pointy goatee and the scar through one eyebrow. He watched me with this creeper smirk on his face that sent a shiver down my spine. And not a good one. As I got closer, his tongue snuck out from between his lips. Something slithered under my skin, and I had to fight a shudder. I moved to the far edge of the group, putting as many people as I could between myself and the goatee man, whose eyes never left me.

"Since we're all finally here." The instructor clapped his hands and gave me a look.

Yes, I know I was late. It bothered me, too. I was never late. My belief had always been fifteen minutes early, on time, on time was late. I resisted looking down at my watch, but I already knew what it said. I had checked the time on the way out of the cabin. I was five minutes late. Mostly because I wasn't really sure that I wanted to go snorkeling. Dash had booked it. Probably because he knew that I was going to spend the entire time they were gone in bed if he didn't fill my days with activities. Vix had even gone the extra step and added all of my 'adventures' into my google calendar.

What was wrong with me?

I had just gotten divorced, and now I was pining over three men I would probably never see again after New Year?

I was pathetic.

I was also not listening to anything the instructor said, so when the goatee man sidled up to me with two pairs of swim fins I gave him an inquisitive look.

"We are to form pairs." He held out one pair of fins to me, but I tucked my hands under my elbows, holding myself protectively from his gaze. I looked over at the rest of the group and saw that I was the only one not paired up already. Well, shit. I took a long breath and took the fins from him and stepped back. "I'm Peter." He held out his hand again, now devoid of fins. He licked those thin lips as his eyes roamed over my body, making my stomach twist.

"Faith," I offered as I took another step back.

"Fitting," Peter hummed, his eyes glued to my breasts. I wished that I had worn one of my one-piece suits, but stupid Birdie had to steal them before I left on vacation. Instead I was left with the little red bikini that she had left in its place. The one that Vix told me was his favorite. With Peter's eyes on me, I wanted to retch.

"We should get going." I nodded over to where the rest of the group was getting their fins and goggles on, lined up along a long wooden dock.

"As you wish, pretty Faith."

Oh vomit.

I hurried to catch up to the rest of the group, nearly tripping over the edge of the dock where it was partially hidden under the sand. Peter's arm snaked around my waist to keep me upright, and I would have rather face-planted than felt his clammy skin on my body. I gave him a quick thanks and shrugged off his arm.

The snorkel tour was a complete blur. I know I took some pictures for Cupid, but I couldn't tell you what they were. Peter took any and all opportunities to touch me, and I couldn't wait until I could go back to my cabin. As empty as it was, it would be preferable to the slimy man's presence.

Cupid

Leaving Faith before dawn was possibly the hardest thing that I had ever done. I left the camera I bought her on the table, hoping that she would remember to take it. That she would actually do the activities we had set up for her.

Vix had even reserved her our table at the restaurant for Christmas dinner. I had never resented my calling as much as I did when the three of us closed her cabin door and headed off to the farthest cove of the island where no one would see us change.

I shed my clothes and tossed them to Dash as he stuffed his own in a bag. Wiggling my shoulders, I hummed to myself as I called my animal.

"Seriously, dude." Dash rolled his eyes at me and dropped the bag behind some rocks for when we got back. "Are you humming that stupid rhyme?"

"What? You have your methods, I have mine." I hummed a few more bars and looked over at Dash and Vix, who were both looking at me. "Fuck off." I growled before I let the animal take my skin.

"At least he doesn't click his heels together and say there's no place like home," Vix commented before letting his own animal out.

"It was one time," Dash grumbled and changed while we waited. *You know, flying commercial would be less strenuous.* Dash's thoughts came through my mind loud and clear.

All those smells stuffed in a tin can? Vix pawed at the ground, obviously eager to get going. He was right; it was a long flight, and we were on a time crunch. *No, thank you.*

Plus, there aren't any direct flights to the North Pole. I rolled my shoulders, mindful of my antlers, and took three long strides before the air solidified under my hooves, and I was airborne. *The general's waiting.* I threw over my shoulder as I gained height.

On Dasher, on Dancer. On Prancer and Vixen. Dash sang obnoxiously.

Oh shut up, asshole. I lengthened my stride, determined to be the first to touch down once we made it home.

On Comet, on Cupid. On Donder and Blitzen. Vix chimed in as they gained on me.

You gonna do the whole thing? Seriously? It was going to be a long flight.

To the top of the perch. To the top of the wall! Dash's voice sang out clear as a bell, even though I had put a good mile between us. My legs burned as I pushed myself harder.

Now dash away, dash away all! I finished the rhyme and shook my head, clearing the first level of clouds that dotted the early morning sky. *Bet I get there first!*

9

Faith

Christmas was exactly how I thought it would be. Lonely.

I sat at the table I had shared with the guys for the last week, and slowly stirred my cranberries into my potatoes, not in the mood for festive. I sagged down in my seat and grabbed my wine glass. I tipped it to my lips and took a gulp of the sweet white wine. I was usually a dry, white kind of girl, preferring Prosecco to a Reisling, but when the waitress - the one who hated me - poured my glass, I hadn't been paying attention, and was stuck with it. After the third glass, I didn't even pretend to try to correct her. I just let the syrupy wine flow like water over my tongue and drifted into the land of the delightfully tipsy.

I planted the glass back on the table, perhaps harder than I intended, 'cause the couple at the next table gave me a look, and pulled my napkin from my lap. I swayed a little as I stood, but I was fine. Totally fine. The fact that I needed to steady myself on a few chairs as I made my way to the door was due to the dining room unexpectedly tilting.

The beach was no less slanted, but I refused to crawl back to my cabin, so I resorted to holding my arms out to keep my balance. God, I wished the boys were with me. Cupid would give me a piggyback ride, or Vix would carry me like a princess. And Dash? Dash would kiss me until I didn't know up from down, and the topsy-turvy ground would mean nothing.

"You seem to be a bit inebriated." A shiver ran down my spine as Peter hooked my arm over his shoulder. I tried to pull away, but he grabbed my hand and held me there.

"Let go of me." I twisted and tugged at my arm fixed across his shoulder. "Please."

"Your mates can't help you now." He leaned close, his sickly breath feathering over my ear. "I have a bit of a score to settle with those three and their boss."

"What are you talking about?" His arm clasped around my waist as he hauled me against his chest, the thick ridge of his cock pressed into my belly as he twisted my ponytail around his hand and pulled. "Please let me go."

"Oh sweetheart," Peter hissed against my lips before he crushed his mouth over mine. I could taste blood as he pulled away. "It's time I take what's theirs. They have already taken so much from me."

"You're crazy." I tried to pull out of his hold, but his arms were like a vice around my body.

"Say goodnight, little Faith." He pushed a rag over my face, the sweet scent of the fabric cloyed at the back of my throat, before everything around me dimmed. "They will give me what I want to get you back, my sweet." I felt my body being surrounded by something, and then the world went dark.

Dash

I flung the door to Faith's cabin open, giddy at the thought of being back with her. Christmas had been stressful. It always was. But we managed to get to every house, to eat all the cookies - little known secret? Santa never ate the cookies, the misses would have his head if he took in that much sugar in one night - and with a little magic, no one was ever the wiser that we had been there.

I dropped the bag of gifts on the kitchen table and looked around the quiet cabin. Weird. We had planned no activities for Faith the afternoon after Christmas, so it was presumed she would be in the cabin.

"Honey," I cupped my hands around my mouth and called out. "We're home." I waited.

Nothing.

"Think she went to the beach?" Cupid fell into one of the living room chairs and kicked his sandy feet up onto the table.

"We should have seen her on the way in then." Vix ducked his head into the bedroom. "The bed has been made."

"So?" The resort's housekeeping staff was impeccable. They practically made the beds before we got out of them.

"No maid service today." Vix pointed at a little note the staff had left on the table. "Which means she hasn't slept in the bed since we left."

"Maybe she stayed in our cabin?" I didn't want to panic, but I could feel that something was wrong. "Are her clothes here?"

"Yep." Cupid called from the closet in the bedroom. "Just a couple things are missing. Her red bikini's in the bathroom."

"Go check out our cabin." Vix whipped out his cell phone and pulled up a call. "I'm getting a hold of the general."

"Dude." I grabbed the phone from him. "Don't call Santa the day after Christmas." I ended the call and stuck the phone in my own pocket. "Did you learn nothing from Rudy's stupid ass, when he walked in on things that should never be spoken of?"

"We all need a little downtime." Vix held out his hand for his phone, but I crossed my arms over my chest. "Weren't we just planning on celebrating a successful mission with our *own* mate?"

"It's like thinking about my parents banging." I shuddered and headed towards the door, snatching up the bag of gifts as I went. "Let's just find her. Calling the general is a last resort."

Our cabin was equally empty. And when we checked with the staff about the activities we had booked for Faith, they said she had only showed up to snorkeling and Christmas Eve dinner.

"Nothing on Christmas Day?" I rubbed my hand over my face and that feeling that something was wrong had turned into a full-blown panic attack centered directly in my stomach. "She really wanted to decorate gingerbread palm trees."

Cupid snorted, but then his face fell. "She wanted to put lights on them," he said soberly. "She was going to leave them for us when we got back."

"I would have noticed gingerbread dicks on the kitchen counter." Vix held out his hand to me, and I dropped his cell into it.

"Time to call the Claus." Fuck.

"Do I point out now or later that I haven't seen Sourpuss today either?" Cupid sat on the sand, shredding the dinner menu that he had snagged while we were chatting with the dining staff. "Cause it can't be a coincidence that Krampus was here, at the resort we always come to, and now Faith's missing."

"That's really not good." I hadn't thought about that. "He wouldn't have done anything. He knows Santa would call in all the troops if one of our mates was taken."

"Perhaps that's exactly what he wants." Vix raised a brow as he put his phone to his ear. "Why don't you check and see if Peter Black has checked out?"

"On it." Cupid and I jumped to our feet and made a dash to the concierge desk in the lobby. I crossed my fingers that Krampus wasn't responsible.

Faith

My mouth felt like it was filled with cotton. And rotten grapes. And cotton soaked in rotten grapes. I rolled over on the bed, my entire body sore. When I pried my eyes open, I was not in my cabin. I wasn't even at the resort. The floor was a slab of concrete with a drain in the middle, and the windows were barred and set high on the wall. And it was definitely too cold to be in the Caribbean. The mattress I lay on was made of straw and looked like it belonged on the set of some slasher film, which did nothing for the anxiety that was crawling up my throat.

"Hello?" I called, then instantly regretted it. What was I always yelling at those stupid blondes in the horror movies Gavin used to make us watch for date night? And that should have been another red flag. Fuck. I rolled off the mattress and breathed in slowly through my mouth as my stomach roiled with the movement.

I waited for the room to stop spinning and carefully got to my feet. I tried to peek through the windows, but they were caked over in filth that I didn't dare touch. A single naked bulb lit the room, leaving harsh shadows against the walls, and I could hear the slow drip of water from somewhere. I didn't even want to check out the deeply shadowed corners, cause I did not want to find a spider. Just the thought sent shivers skittering up my spine.

Everything about that room made my skin crawl. It was all very not good. Bad. It was very, very bad. I looked at my watch. But the crystal was cracked, and the hands were not moving. I tried to be upset about that, but it had been an anniversary present from Gavin's mother. The same woman who congratulated my ex-husband when we left the lawyer's office after signing the divorce papers. I think her exact words were 'I never liked her anyhow. I'm glad you left before you accidentally knocked her up.' Toxic bitch. I pulled the watch band off my wrist and tossed it in the corner with the spiders. Yeah, the ones that weren't there. Gah, yuck.

The door was my next mission. I had no doubt that it was locked, but maybe I could have jimmied it open. Unlikely.

I pulled at the handle a few times, and rattled the door, but it barely budged. It was solid wood, and in the damp it had expanded into the frame tightly. I probably couldn't have even gotten it open if it wasn't locked. Defeated, I slid down to the floor and banged my head against the concrete wall.

What I couldn't figure out: why was I even in a basement room to begin with?

I had no significance. There was no one to ransom me. My parents were long dead, my ex-husband couldn't care less, and as I had already established, his mother wasn't going to cry any tears over me. So why me?

Peter had said something about my mates, right?

Did that make him a terrorist or something? That's who would kidnap military family members. I guess. But I wasn't. I was their Christmas Holiday fling. I know they had said all that stuff about mating for life, and the perfect mate, but that's what guys said. I had no delusions about that. If I ever got out of whatever I was in, I was going home. Alone.

The sound of footsteps against concrete had me on my feet in an instant. I backed away from the door as far as I could get. And waited.

10

Vix

There was no mission report to devour. No preparation. Just waiting. "I'm going to go search Krampus's cabin." I jumped to my feet and grabbed my pack. A little breaking and entering would be nothing. It was all a part of the Claus magic that we all were infused with when we entered the service. Who knew when you would have to step up and take over for the general. We all had to be prepared to carry out the mission no matter what.

"What's that gonna tell you, man?" Cupid sat at the dining table of Faith's cabin twisting one of her hair tie things in his fingers. "I imagine he packed up and you know. . ." He put his finger to the side of his nose. "Poofed out."

"He could have missed something." I hooked my bag over my shoulder and marched out. Fucking Peter Black hadn't checked out. That was the first thing we checked. But he certainly wasn't on the island. We had canvassed the beaches, and none of the waitstaff had seen him at meals since Christmas Eve. "Please, have missed something," I whispered to myself as I stalked up to the cabin door and pulled my bag around to pull out the tool I needed to hack the electronic lock on the door. "There's got to be a trace we can follow."

Upon first look, the cabin seemed to be empty of any personal effects. But a second sweep brought a cell phone that had slid under the bed. I pressed the power button, but the phone was dead. Not surprising since it had been sitting unplugged under a bed for two days.

I tucked the phone into my pocket and gave the cabin one last run through, but found nothing else.

It was something, at least.

I jogged back to the cabin to find a charger for the phone. Likelihood was that it was Faith's, since Krampus would have noticed his missing. I held the phone aloft as I burst back into the cabin. "Someone grab me a charger." I dumped my bag on the floor and waited for Dash to hand me the charger. Once the phone was plugged in, it was just a matter of waiting for it to charge long enough for it to be turned on.

Message after message flooded the screen. Each and every one was from Birdie. I went to see if I could unlock the phone when a call brightened up the screen. I swiped my thumb to accept the call and put it on speaker.

"There better be a fantastic reason as to why you haven't returned any of my calls for two days!" The irate woman on the other end growled. "I've been worried sick."

"Birdie, I presume?" I tipped the phone so that the others could hear.

"Who the fuck is this?" It made my heart glad that my mate had such a fierce best friend. "And what have you done to my Faith?"

"Sadly, I do not have any answers." I set the phone down on the table and paced around the room. "As to who I am? I am Vixen Hallewell. It is certainly a pleasure to make your acquaintance, Birdie. Though I fear that it is not the best of circumstances."

"Where's Faith?" Birdie seemed to have subdued quite a bit.

"I fear she may have been abducted."

"The fuck you say!" Birdie's voice hit a decibel I'm sure only dogs, and unfortunately shifters, could hear, but I understood her anxiety. "She's on an island, how did she get abducted?"

"The how is still being deduced." I told her carefully, eyeing my brothers. "But rest assured, we are on it."

"Oh, you're on it, are you?" My mate's best friend was fantastic. "What the fuck are you going to do?"

"I assure you that we have the skills in which to bring Faith home again." There was a sharp knock at the door, before it opened, and in walked the general.

"I need a sitrep, where are we with Krampus?" Santa rolled the sleeves of his fatigue shirt up his forearms, displaying his thickly inked skin. "I have boots on the ground in Germany, Austria, and Hungary. I can't imagine my brother would stray far from his old stomping grounds."

"Ex-nay on the Ampus-Kray," Cupid pointed at the phone with wide eyes. "Birdie, we're going to have to call you back."

"Nope." We can hear Birdie smack something, I assume it was the table, as it gave a wooden thump as her hand struck it. "Tell me what's going on. Faith is my responsibility. I'm her best friend."

"I assure you Bernadine Yeats Spankmeyer, Faith Amanda Cox nee Greathouse, is in expert hands with my men and I." Santa gave me his little secret wink and picked up the phone off the table. "She will be home before you know it, and you can give her that kitten you found for her."

"Okay. . . that's just creepy."

"Santa knows all, my dear." He looked at each of us in turn. "Now, as much of a pleasure as it is for us to chat, I think we can all agree that finding Faith is our top priority."

"I can understand knowing my name; you all are military types. I'm sure you ran a background check, but how do you know I got her a kitten?" Birdie asked quietly.

"I promise to tell you when we bring Faith home," was all Santa said before ending the call.

"She's just going to call back." Dash raised a brow at the general, who just laid his finger along his nose and winked. Then his phone dinged. "It seems we have a location." He held up his phone. Bad Wimpfen, it looked like we were headed for Germany.

Faith

The footsteps stopped before they reached the door and retreated again. I could hear a door slamming deeper in the house, but then there was silence. I tucked my knees up to my chin on the straw mattress against the wall and watched the door. It was a long time before I heard anything else, and by that time the light that filtered through the filthy windows had waned, and my eyes were heavy.

My growling stomach was the only sound I could hear as my eyes drifted closed, but chaos exploded through the house moments later. Silence had reigned the entire time I had been awake, and now, suddenly, the world was awash with noise.

I pressed my back to the wall and pulled the poor excuse for a mattress up as far as it would go. It was little more than a sack of muslin filled with sharp barbs of straw, and it sagged as I tried to pull it onto its side, but it was all I had. I sat huddled under the straw, the cold from the concrete seeping into my skin when the door burst open. I could see splinters wrenched from the frame tumble to the floor as the door slammed against the wall and Peter stood there.

"You have proven to be a problem." He stalked towards me, ripping the mattress from my grip with ease, and locking his long fingers around my throat. "It seems the cavalry has arrived. Sadly, your mates are not among them, and thus you have outlived your usefulness."

He pulled me to my feet, his fingers digging into my neck until I was fighting for air. I tried to pull his arm free, but he just squeezed tighter. He lifted until my toes barely touched the floor.

"You see." He slammed me against the wall with a force that made my bones rattle. My head spun where it connected. I tore at his fingers around my neck, my lungs screaming for air, but his grip was like a vice. My nails tore as I dug them into his skin, but he didn't even flinch. "I was meant to run the Alpha Team." He shook me, slamming me again into the wall and the world tilted. "I was the generals second in command, and then Vixen came." Peter pulled me away from the wall, his nose pressed right against mine, his breath bathing my face as my lungs worked, trying to bring in that oxygen he was carelessly wasting against my skin. "Vixen and then Dasher, and finally your precious Cupid. Meddling fuckers digging into everything." He tossed me at the floor like I was nothing but a rag doll. My head cracked against the concrete and my vision blurred. "They stole my birthright. So, I will take their mate." I closed my eyes, not wanting to see what he had in store for me next. The flash of something in the bulb's light above us seared into my mind as I squeezed my eyes shut.

I heard two pops. Then nothing.

Cupid

Faith's fingers were so limp in my hand as I listened to the steady beat of her heart monitor. I lay my head on the mattress near our linked hands and let out what was probably my first full breath in a day. "The doctors say you're going to be fine," I told my sleeping mate. "They've given you some medication for your head, it's making you sleep. We worried a lot about you, Faith." I ran my fingers over her knuckles, wishing she would wake up, that her fingers would lace with mine, and my heart would be whole again. "Birdie's been blowing up your phone. She heard a few things that were classified, and now she's freaking out. The general and Dash went to go pick her up. But she's gonna have a lot of questions, like about how you got to Germany, and why we're at the North Pole, and about Santa, and you know, if there really are elves, you know, all kinds of things we should have told you before we left." I sighed and tipped my head towards the head of the bed, just watching her lashes flutter against her cheeks.

"Hey man," Donder leaned in the doorway, a cup of coffee in his hand. "The general's back."

"Send Birdie back when he's done talking to her, yeah?"

"Can do." He handed me the coffee mug and knocked on the door frame before waving his goodbye.

"You said your job was mobile, right?" I set the mug on the nightstand to cool and brushed a hair off Faiths cheek. "'Cause we would really like it if you would stay here with us." I sat back in my chair and ran my hands over my face. Three day's worth of scruff tickled my palms. "We have so much to tell you, baby girl."

11

Faith

Waking up in a small hospital room in Germany was a bit of a shock. But all three of my boys were there waiting for me. Cupid had fallen asleep with his head on my bed, one hand laced with mine, While Vix sat reading in a chair and Dash had his feet up on the coffee table and was sprawled out all over the couch. They hovered for the entire two days I was in the hospital, and then insisted on taking me back to my house in Vermont. A ride in Santa's actual slay was a shock to say the least. The big man himself? Yeah, he did not have a bowl full of jelly for a middle. He was just as ripped as my guys, a little older, but fuck was Santa a silver fox if I ever met one.

My house was exactly as I left it. The rooms felt empty now that Gavin had collected his things while I was on vacation. The cupboards were nearly bare without the china we had been given for our wedding, and his grandmother's silver.

"You know, we can help you pack." Dash lounged at my kitchen table with one of my novelty mugs in his hand that said 'Hakuna Mafuckit.' Birdie had gotten it for me for a birthday years ago. My mugs were some of the only dishes left in the house. Those and the coffee maker were absolutely mine. "Just say the world."

"Pack?" I sat down next to him with my own novelty mug filled with steaming hot nectar of the Gods. I took a long breath, pulling the rich earthy scent of coffee into my lungs. Even when you fly the Santa Express - and seriously it took like fifteen minutes to get home - pulled by your sexy mates, jet lag was a real thing. "Where am I going?"

"Home." Cupid dropped a kiss on my head and sat down, his feet going up on the table with a thud. "We talked about this."

"We talked about the fact that mates means forever." I looked down into my mug, wondering if it was cool enough yet to drink. I was going to need caffeine for a talk about moving in with three men I had really just met.

"And we also talked about how we live up at the North Pole, how we would like you to join us there." Vix had unearthed a box of tea in my cupboard that had to be five years out of date, but I wasn't going to argue with him. He wanted tea. "You agreed. Your job is mobile, no reason not to live with us."

"Birdie." I argued. I couldn't leave my best friend. "She's my person."

"Love." Vix tucked a stray hair behind my ear and his fingers lingered against my cheek. I leaned into his hand, the scent of Christmas wafting over me. Just a single touch and I forgot my entire argument. "We can visit. But we need you with us."

"Okay," I agreed, rubbing my face against his hand. They were home. I knew that, but with all the changes that had taken over my life, leaving Birdie would be next to impossible. "I want to visit often."

"We have plenty of missions throughout the year." Dash shrugged and drained his mug. He took long strides to the coffee pot and refilled his cup. "Anytime we'll be away, we can bring you back here first."

"If I'm leaving, I should sell the house." I looked around the opened planned first floor of the house I had bought with a man who was gone. And that hole in my heart that he had left when he walked away? It didn't burn anymore. It was just a small ache. It had been his house. He had wanted one in the city instead of out in the country like I wanted. He wanted to be close to work. "I want to sell the house. It's not really mine anymore."

"Sounds like a plan." Cupid bounced to his feet and ran into the next room. He came back with an arm full of boxes. "Last one the the lingerie drawer has to wear whatever is in there." And then he was gone again.

"He's gonna be really disappointed," I said into my mug.

"I like you naked best, anyhow." Dash pulled me into his lap and cuddled me as we both drank our coffee.

Dash

I dropped the last of Faith's boxes into the garage and sat down heavily on the step leading into the house. "The house looked so empty." I leaned back against the door and looked around. "Where did all this stuff come from?"

Faith sat down next to me, looking super cute in her puffy coat and fuzzy mittens. Summer at the North Pole was still wicked cold. She would get used to it. "It is a lot." She looked around and found the box labeled 'kitchen' and pulled it down. "For now, I want coffee and I want my mugs."

"Mrs. Claus is having us for dinner in a few hours." I followed her into the kitchen and watched her unpack her coffee maker. "The guys wanted to have some Faith time before Annette steals you away."

"Oh?" Faith looked over her shoulder, her eyes already starting to dilate. "And what do you boys have in mind?"

I wrapped my arms around her waist and threw her over my shoulder. She squealed, but hugged my hips as I carried her out of the kitchen and up the steps towards the master bedroom. "I think we need to christen the house." I dropped her down on the bed and pulled off her shoes.

"I think that's an excellent idea," she giggled as she stripped off her coat and mittens, throwing them onto the floor. "Are the others joining? Or is it just you and me?"

"Oh baby, we're gonna all be walking in an orgasm wonderland." Cupid walked in and threw his shirt on the floor next to the ever growing pile of clothes that Faith and I had been making.

"Yes please." Faith lifted her hips so I could pull off her jeans. I took her panties with them and looked down at my naked mate. Fuck she was beautiful. "I want you all stuffing my stockings." She licked her lips and reached toward me, pulling me onto the bed with her. "I wanna lick your candy cane first, though." She pushed me down and settled between my legs.

"Now that is a sight." I could see Vixen leaning in the doorway, his eyes on our mate's upturned ass. "Cupid, why don't you make sure she's ready for us."

"You don't have to tell me twice." He crawled up the mattress behind Faith and ducked down. I knew the moment his mouth hit her pussy, 'cause her entire face reflected ecstasy. "Fuck you taste like sugar plums."

"Faith, I believe you are leaving Dash hanging." Vix settled himself on the armchair next to the bed. Naked, he held his cock in his hand. "If you're going to ride me like a reindeer, you better get to work on his North Pole."

Faith wrapped her hand around the base of my cock and rolled her eyes up to look at me as she licked around the head, her tongue teasing the ridge just under the crown before she took me between those sweet lips. I let her get me nice and wet, she moans vibrating through me as Cupid worked her pussy. When her hips started rocking back against his face, I sunk my hands into her hair and pulled her down over my cock. I hit the back of her throat, and felt it relax around me. Fuck. I wasn't going to last long once I watched her lips touch her fingers still wrapped around the base. She tightened her hand and followed her lips up my dick as she hollowed out her cheeks.

"Just like that, baby." I growled as she licked the tip of my cock and then sank back down without any prompting. Her hips rocked erratically against Cupid. I could feel her orgasm bubbling, her throat tightening around me. "You want me to cum in your mouth?" Her hum was all I needed. I gripped her hair and pulled her down as far as I knew she could go, and let my release wash over me. My girl swallowed everything I gave her, then licked me clean with a satisfied look on her face. "Fuck. I love you, Faith."

"Love you too, Dash." She dropped a kiss on the skin just above my cock. "Cupid?" She looked over her shoulder at my friend, who was sitting back on his heels. "You gonna get that present into my box, or am I going to have to ask Vix to do it for you?"

"Lay down, babe." Cupid helped her lay down on her back between my legs, her shoulders resting in my lap. He crawled over her and kissed her, her release still painting his face. "I wanna watch you this time." He lined himself up with her and pushed in. Her back arched as he filled her, her hair tickling my chest. I gathered it in my hand and wrapped it around my fist, pulling just a little.

"Cupid," she moaned, wrapping her legs around his hips as he lifted her into his lap and drove into her. "Harder." I pulled her hair a little more and she moaned. "Dash, please." Her chest lifted as she looked up at me. "I need more." I kept the pressure on her hair and reached down with my other hand to pull at her nipples. The harder I pinched the more she thrashed under Cupid. Her eyes rolled in her head, and she tensed. "Oh God." Her body shuddered against me, and my dick started to come back to life. "Dash, you gonna fuck me, too?" She sagged under Cupid as he roared with his release. He dropped down and pulled the nipple I wasn't torturing into his mouth.

"Vix gets to go first." I unwound her hair from my hand. "I think he wants you to go sit in his lap." Faith turned her head and looked over to where Vix was sitting. One hand on his cock, the other had a long red ribbon.

"Come to me, Faith." Something flashed in Vixon's eyes, and I knew he had a game in mind for our mate. "I want you sitting on my dick, while Dash prepares you for another cock."

"Please," Faith whined and slid out from between us and onto the floor. She crawled to Vix, Cupid's cum dripping out of her. "Make me full." She licked the pre-cum off the tip of Vix's cock before pulling herself up and kneeling over him. He pulled her hips down over him, impaling her on his cock, then gathering her hands behind her and winding the ribbon expertly around her wrists.

Faith

Vix knotted my hands behind me and tested the bond before he pulled me against his chest. "You ready for two of us, sweetheart?" He held my hips down against him, so all I could do was squirm with his cock buried deep inside me. My movements earned me a stinging smack against my ass. "I asked you a question, little one."

"Yes," I breathed as Vix rubbed the sting from my ass, then smacked the other cheek just as hard.

"Yes, what?" he purred against my ear.

"Yes, please Vix." I wanted him to move, for him to make me feel good, but he just held me down.

"Good girl." He captured my lips in an all consuming kiss so I barely noticed the second set of hands rubbing up and down my arms. "Dash, I believe you wanted something from our girl?"

"I want your ass, baby." Dash's hands replaced Vix's on my hips before he ran his fingers between the globes of my ass, pulling them apart, his thumb pressing into my most secret place. "Would you like that?"

I had never let Gavin touch my ass. It hadn't ever felt right, but the way that the pad of Dash's thumb was caressing the tight bud, all I could think of was him pressing inside of me, filling me even further. I wanted him. I wanted him to take my ass and leave his cum inside of me.

"Please Dash," I looked over my shoulder and locked eyes with my beautiful green eyed mate. "Fuck my ass."

"Let's get you ready first, love." Vix gave me one shallow thrust of his cock, making my insides clench around him. "Just relax."

The pop of a cap, then cool liquid ran down my crack, meeting Dash's thumb. He rubbed the lube against my bud lazily. At first it felt strange, but as I relaxed I found that I couldn't wait for him to breach the ring of muscle. He did, slowly. First the tip of his thumb, then he retreated. "More," I whined, which earned me a sharp smack from Vix.

"Patience." Vix pressed a biting kiss to my lips, and I chased it, losing myself in the feel of Vix inside me, and his lips against mine, with Dash slowly opening me, an gettin me ready for his cock. I wanted his cock so badly by the time he slipped a second finger in with the first, scissoring them apart.

"Vix." I pulled my lips from his. "I'm ready, please. I want you both inside of me."

Vix nodded to Dash, who pulled his fingers from my ass. Just that small retreat made me whine. I needed them both inside of me, I was too empty without Dash. But he was already there, pressing the blunt head of his cock against my virgin hole. I breathed out and relaxed as the head penetrated. A sharp pain was soothed as soon as the head popped through the muscle ring, and then he slid right in.

"Oh Gods." I bit into Vix's shoulder as I adjusted to the new intrusion. I felt so full. "It's too much."

"Just relax baby," Dash soothed as he petted my back, leaving kisses on my shoulders, my bound arms pressed between us. And then began to move. Ecstasy flowed through my veins. "Faith, baby, you're so tight."

"More." I couldn't breath. The pleasure was spiraling so high. "I need more, please."

"Cupid?" Vix called to my final mate. "I believe that our Faith needs you as well."

"It would be my genuine pleasure." I turned my head and watched Cupid stroll across the floor to us, his hand pulling languidly at his cock as he watched me being fucked by his two best friends. "You need me babe?" I nodded my head and rolled my eyes uI could look in his eyes as he pressed the head of his dick against my lips. "Open wide." He pressed into my mouth slowly. "Can I be in charge, sweetness? You gonna let me fuck that mouth, while Dash and Vix fuck you?"

"Please," I said as he pulled his cock from between my lips.

"You look at me." Cupid grabbed a fist full of my hair and stretched my head back to him. He pressed back into my mouth pushing until I could feel him in my throat. "Don't let those eyes leave mine," he growled as he pulled back almost all the way. I licked around the head of his cock before he thrust back into my throat.

Vix's hips hitched against mine, and I could feel him wiggle his fingers between us. When his thumb pressed against my clit, my world whited out. I was lost in the sensations of my three mates claiming me as one. My orgasm swept over me like a tidal wave, extending forever as I felt my mates cum inside me, filling me until I was bursting.

Cupid's cock slipped from between my lips, and his thumb rubbed against my bottom lip, where I had made a bit of a mess. He pressed his thumb into my mouth to be licked clean. "You are so beautiful like this, babe."

Cupid helped me up, sweeping me into his arms when my legs gave out under me and carried me to the bathroom.

"How about a hot bath, relax those sore muscles." Dash was already drawing the bathe when he asked.

"Only if you join me." I smiled at Dash as Cupid set me gently into the hot water.

"Don't have to ask me twice." Both boys crawled into the huge master bath tub and cuddled around me. I let my head fall against Cupid's shoulder. The warm water swirling around us lulled me off to sleep within moments.

EPILOGUE

Faith

One Year Later

Who would have imagined that taking my second honeymoon on my own would lead to finding three amazing men, getting kidnapped by what I thought was a fictional character, or me finding my real happily ever after?

I sat looking out at the beach from my little cabin, and rested my hand on my still mostly flat stomach, watching for the boys to return from their daily run. Yep, I couldn't be happier. Living in the North Pole had taken a minor adjustment. Days and nights are very different when you live at the very top of the world, and trying to figure out time zones when it comes to attending client meetings proved to be a bit of a headache. But I was settled, and enjoying a post-Christmas vacation on the beach with my mates.

So, I would never get to spend Christmas day with them. Who cared? I spent it with Mrs. Claus, who is delightful, and my best friend Birdie, who had recently made the big move to the North Pole as well, but then her story is for a different time.

Cupid came jogging up to the cabin, his shirt tucked into the waistband of his trunks, and a gleeful grin splitting his handsome face. "You're up." He stopped and bent to lay a kiss on my upturned face. His lips are salty but soft. "We didn't want to wake you. You need your beauty sleep for this one." He held his palm over my hand where it lay on my belly. "Good morning, little one. You be good to your momma this morning."

"I think we've hit the end of the morning sickness." I accepted another kiss from my mate, with a smile on my face. "At least I hope so."

"I love you, momma." Cupid nuzzled his nose against mine and stole another kiss.

"I love you from head to mistletoe, Cupid."

THE END

ACKNOWLEDGMENTS

My lovely readers,

This will probably be the one and only Christmas story you get from me. I wrote it back in 2020 when I was desperately trying to find a way to be creative during the first lockdown of the pandemic. I wanted nothing else but to get something out of myself that was just pure escapism during a time when I was scared that nothing would ever be the same again.

Originally this was for a Christmas anthology that ended up falling apart at the end. Tremendously sad that I wouldn't get to share this little bright spot with all of you, I turned to my lovely book wife Miri Stone (back before we were book wives!). As with all things Miri and I, it quickly snowballed from "what am I doing with this story" to "of course we should make an entire anthology around it and gather all of our friends to play on our crazy train."

So, in a month and a half, somehow we pulled together our first ever anthology Christmas Nibbles. I made my first cover, we found our first charity, and by some Christmas Miracle we pulled a rabbit out of a hat, and published not only on time, but with some pretty incredible reception.

It was an amazing, if not extraordinarily stressful, experience. Since we have moved on to Halloween anthologies with our friends Mariah, Shelly and Kess, but the things that we learned that first year still hang on. And Christmas Nibbles and the stories that were a part of it will aways hold a special place in our hearts.

Back to the story. While it was a huge amount of fun to write, Christmas—lets be honest—isn't really my holiday, being Jewish and not really celebrating. I hope you enjoy Faith and her mates, and as always, leaving a review helps each and every author a tremendous amount and also helps other readers discover our books. So, if you are so inclined, please consider leaving one on your store of choice or on your favorite social media platform.

XOXO,

Kat

P.S.—If you're curious about more of my books, or are looking to get updated on the crazy things I get up to (spoiler - its really just my characters who find all the drama) you can jump over to my website or my newsletter for more up to date goings on in all my worlds!

ABOUT THE AUTHOR

If you're looking for steamy paranormal romance, you've come to the right place. K.O. Newman writes everything from gods and monsters to fairies and shifters.

When she's not immersed in her own fantasy world, K.O. is a mom to two little boys, and wife to a fantastic man. She lives outside of St. Louis in southern Illinois, and spends her days working with seniors at a retirement community.

Writing is in her bones. K.O. has been toiling with stories since she was old enough to hold a book, despite struggling with dyslexia. She started writing fanfiction in highschool, and quickly began to grow her own characters and stories. Her mind is constantly filled with new friends (and steamy book boyfriends) that she can't wait to share.

Check out my Website for more.

If you're looking to keep up with all my releases and what's going on with me and my authoring world, come check me out on Substack!

ALSO BY K.O. NEWMAN

Lords Of Khaos Series

Malachai

Lesleigh

Cherry

Finnegan

Fitzgerald (coming soon)

Standalones

Secret Omega

Reclaiming Psyche

Autumn Curses

Wish

Stupid Cupid

With Mariah Thayer

Blood Moon Riders Series

Crow Moon

Pink Moon

Flower Moon

Hot Moon

Thunder Moon

Omnibus One

Witches of Winter Haven

Wing Witch (Coming Soon)

With Miri Stone

Soul of the Chaos

Bartender Mate (Coming Soon)

With Shelly Ferguson

Ember (Coming Soon)